S0-AUN-913

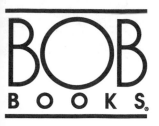

SCHOLASTIC READER
LEVEL 1
50-250 WORDS

Outdoor Adventures!

by LYNN MASLEN KERTELL
illustrated by SUE HENDRA

SCHOLASTIC INC.

New York   Toronto   London   Auckland

Sydney   Mexico City   New Delhi   Hong Kong

No part of this publication may be reproduced, stored in a retrieval system, or transmitted in any form or by any means, electronic, mechanical, photocopying, recording, or otherwise, without written permission of the publisher. For information regarding permission, write to Scholastic Inc., Attention: Permissions Department, 557 Broadway, New York, NY 10012.

ISBN 978-0-545-38271-7

Copyright © 2012 by Lynn Maslen Kertell. All rights reserved. Published by Scholastic Inc. by arrangement with Bob Books® New Initiatives LLC. SCHOLASTIC and associated logos are trademarks and/or registered trademarks of Scholastic Inc. BOB BOOKS and associated logos are trademarks and/or registered trademarks of Bob Books Publications LLC. Lexile® is a registered trademark of MetaMetrics.

10 9 8 7 6 5 4 3 2 1

12 13 14 15 16 17/0

Printed in the U.S.A.   40
First printing, July 2012

"Jack, Jack, Dad will take us on a hike today!" yells Anna.

Anna puts on sunscreen.
Jack runs to the car.

4

Dad brings lunch and drinks.

Jack and Anna sit in the car.
They ride and ride.

They pass the city.
They drive to the country.

"We are here!" says Dad.

Jack and Anna start up the path.

They go under trees.
They cross a stream.

"I see tracks," says Jack.
"Look! Animals!" says Anna.

Dad puts the picnic blanket
on the grass.
"Give that back," says Jack
to the frisky squirrel.

The sun is low.
The air cools down.
It is time to go home.

"I love hiking with you, Dad," says Anna.

"Thanks, Dad!" says Jack
as he gives Dad a hug.

The next day, Jack and Anna
want to go on another hike.

They make a picnic.
They get ready.

Mom says, "Not today, kids."

"Today you can not
go on a hike."

Jack and Anna do not drive in the car

They do not pass the city.

They do not go into the country.

Jack says, "I know
what we can do."

Jack and Anna go in the yard.

Jack and Anna walk up the path.

They go under trees.
They cross a stream.

"Look! Animals!" says Anna.

"I see tracks," says Jack.

27

Anna puts their picnic
blanket on the grass.

"Give that back!" says Jack
to the frisky puppy.

The sun gets low.
The air cools down.

"Come in," calls Mom.

"We made our own hike,"
say Jack and Anna.
"Yes, you did,"
agree Mom and Dad.